How Do You Wokka-Wokka?

Elizabeth Bluemle

illustrated by Randy Cecil

CANDLEWICK PRESS

Some days you wake up
and you just gotta wokka—

Say "HEY!" to your neighbors
up and down the blocka

wammy-lammy-wotcha-hoo.
Do your funky wokka,
get your dance on.

How do you wokka-wokka?

I wokka-wokka
like flamingos
in a flocka–

croakie-yocka

leggy-longy

pinky-hoppa-hoppa

How do you wokka-wokka?

I wokka like a
mariachi with
maracas—

chipi-chipi

chaba-cha-cha

shake-a-the-maracas

Hey, let's wokka-wokka,
shimmy-shake, and shocka-shocka!

Everybody dance now in your
shiny shoes and socka-socka.

You can always wokka
in your own wokka way.

Won't you come out with me
on this fine old wokka day?

How do you wokka-wokka?

I wokka-wokka
like a clock
go ticka-tocka–

pitta-patta

time-no-matta

picka-pocka-ticka-tocka

How
do you
wokka-
wokka?

I wokka-wokka
like a fish flop
on a dock-a–

flip-a-floppa

off-the-docka

put-me-back-in-wata-wata

Hey, let's wokka-wokka,
shimmy-shake, and shocka-shocka!

Time to get a move-on in your
shiny shoes and socka-socka.

Everybody wokka in their
own crazy way.

Won't you wokka with me
on this fine old sunny day?

How do YOU wokka-wokka?

I wokka-wokka
at your door go
knocka-knocka–

rap-bap

biddly-ap

open-up-and-boppa

WE wokka-wokka like
a party on the blocka!

Shacka-racka
daddly-acka

cotton-candy

snacka-snacka.

Nobody wokkas
in the same wokka way.

It's a wokka-wokka party
each and every wokka day!

We all gonna rocka

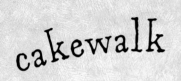

cakewalk

till we droppa.

Yeah, ya gotta wokka!